# HOLDING BACK WINTER

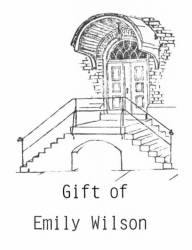

# HOLDING BACK WINTER
## Poems by Judy Goldman

*Judy Goldman*

St. Andrews Press
Laurinburg, NC 28352

NC Women's Expression Series
Margaret Baddour, Editor

I am grateful to the editors of the following journals in which some of these poems first appeared:

*The Arts Journal, Anthology of Magazine Verse & Yearbook of American Poetry, Blue Pitcher, A Carolina Literary Companion, Carolina Quarterly, The Chattahoochee Review, Creative Loafing, The Crescent Review, Crucible, Cumberland Poetry Review, The Davidson Miscellany, The Emrys Journal, The Greensboro Review, Irene Leache Memorial Prize Winners 1985, The Louisville Review, The Lyricist, North Carolina Poetry Society Award-Winning Poems, Outerbridge, Pembroke Magazine, The Pilot, Poem, St. Andrews Review, Southern Poetry Review, Swallow's Tale, The Texas Review, Thunder & Honey, Uwharrie Review, The Wayah Review, The Wilmington Review,* and *The Worcester Review.*

Copyright ©1987 Judy Goldman
First published 1987
ISBN 0-932662-64-1
Library of Congress Catalog Card No. 87-060961

Published by
St. Andrews Press
St. Andrews Presbyterian College
Laurinburg, NC 28352

Cover design: Jerry Torchia
Printed by Printcrafters of the Carolinas, Inc.
Charlotte, North Carolina

# CONTENTS

## III. HOLDING BACK WINTER

*For my parents — I promised them a book of poetry. And for Henry, Laurie, and Mike, who helped me keep my promise.*

# I. A SUMMER THE SHAPE OF GARDENIAS

# I LIKE TO LOOK IN LIGHTED HOUSES

and memorize the rooms
as I pass by. All that's needed
is a lamp by the window
and shades left up since morning.

Sometimes I see a family
from years ago. The father

hums ah sweet mystery of life
as he shaves upstairs.
The blonde brush. The cup.
The cloudy mirror. And the soap
glazing the sink like a second skin.

There's the mother in the kitchen
watering a row of African violets
which line the double windowsill
like Sunday children.
It must be summer.
Her arms are tanned and I can tell
her nails are polished.

The son is in his room
caught in the spin of old jazz.
A record plays
and notes curl around him
forming a circle as perfect
as a trumpet's brass throat.

I see two daughters in the den
stretched across the rug,
their thin legs making a pattern
like dancers in a water ballet.
They play a game of cards,
their hair falling around their faces.

Walking away, I wave
as if I'd been a week-end guest.
But I want to go back
and enter that glimpse.

I would slip down narrow halls,
switch on a lamp
beside the window in each room,
soft light catching the back of my head
for anyone passing outside.

# NO FOOLISHNESS ABOUT HIM

My father and his solemn monuments
of books. He used giant dictionary words
as if they were small, sure brush strokes
painting a solid curtain. The pages
I wanted to riffle like scarves
in his face, pitch a paisley light
about the room. My father

walked the aisles at work
until the whole store was full of him
and every shelf was lined
with what he knew, the front windows
neon blue with everything he taught.
Ladies' dresses huddled together in racks,
shrinking under his voice into threads
of dry colors. My father

leveled his shoulders into a putt,
shifted his wrists to snap the ball
across the green. I watched him bend his neck
under the weight of countless shots gone wrong
as if the rest of him hung loose
on a wire hanger. I wanted to
pull his arms around me, then pretend
we were dancing. In a dream my father

walks away, that long stride,
and just before I wake, he turns
so I can see the stitches in his hat
clear as I see his smile
and the slightly foolish wink
before it is all over.

## EARLY INNINGS

My father's friends that minor league summer
filled the box with loudspeaker voices
and seersucker trousers. I sat
close enough to Father
to smell his evening cigar, inhale
the infield talk until I was drunk
with striped jerseys, base hits, peanuts
parched in bags. And I was pitcher
hurling fastballs wild to all-star hitters
and striking them out. Lead-off
batter, I scored for my father
with a long, high drive
over the right field fence,
over all fences. My father smiled,
called me safe at home.

One midseason game I strutted new sandals,
straps braiding bird legs
like a trellis on sunburn. I had to curl
all ten toes to see those scenes
painted beneath bare feet,
flamingos on my soles, awkward as girls.
The game was called for rain. My sandals bled
rosy puddles after only one inning
as I half-ran mud and water,
dark fields behind the park
to keep up with Father's strides
all the way back to our '52 Olds.

## BITE-SIZE PIECES

Without my mother,
who will cut up the world
into bite-size pieces for me?

—*Enchantment*
by Daphne Merkin

1.

She is painting my knee orange,
dipping her wand again and again
in the small brown bottle. Mercurochrome.
A word that sits on the edge of my tongue
like music. I sing its syllables
until they are soundless.

2.

My mother pours cups of warm water
through my hair until the strands
are dark as school nights
and the last bubble of shampoo
becomes a thin line
marking the porcelain.
My forehead is buried
in a folded washcloth
on the edge of the kitchen sink.
I could be praying. I could be
learning how black and white linoleum
eventually turns liquid
beneath bare feet.

3.

My mother plays the piano
while I dance, the tips of my shoes
winking at her in the muted light
of late afternoon. Her chords
measure the room, bringing the walls in
around me like arms.

.    .    .    .

She reduced it all
as if the whole world
were her dressing table
and the glass-topped bottles
on her mirrored tray
held delicious certainties
the colors of spice.
As if the whole world
were a handbag she could reach inside,
taking out the one thing I needed.

# I'VE ALWAYS BEEN LIGHT AS CELLOPHANE

In the muscle of childhood it was
Red Rover, that game of colliding
strength. My wrist still stings
from Irene Brunson, her full side flung
at me as if I were an Oriental rug
to beat, raising dust from pores.
Fingers clutched fingers
even after my hollow arm snapped.

Pounds are not what I am talking about.
Do you weigh a moth's wing? Measure
wisteria? Maybe you have seen me
memorize the ground, slipping higher,
helium spinning through my veins.

Inching backwards up the seesaw
I followed a cousin's instructions
solid as her frame, trying to balance
her body and mine.
Everything was pattern
as she pulled me to my feet
from hard-packed dirt. My legs
thin strands of rope tangled.

At least I know my own weight now.
And still I float, a speck of ash
that stubbornly remains
long after fire has had the breath
knocked out of it.

## SMALL TOWN DANCER

Turn turn turn
starched light catches
the down on my young legs
twisting me in piqué circles
across the room. Toe shoes spin
satin halos, snap
the dust at
Van Tassel School of Dance
behind Ed Allen's Grocery.
People weighing their grapes
hear the music
Miss Dotson makes
with her thin-skinned fingers
and upright piano.
I am spinning, reeling,
dancing to please Miss Van Tassel,
to keep time to the music.
I slip across the floor
like ribbon
untying perfectly
inch by inch.

## HOOTCHY KOOTCHY

Walking backwards
down the midway I snatched
one last look

to catch twin tassels  as long as a man's
finger
spinning garter belt dreams, twirling
small circles
around each perfect
breast, those rings
circling my neck, yanking
me back to see how she spun

one to the East        the other to the West.

Lips tattooed across her face
sucked one and all through the flaps
inside the smoky tent
to let the breeze
she gave rise to

nip the air,
roll over their faces
like somebody's flesh.

## THOSE LADIES

Not that we ever saw one.

Still, those nights
our '56 Ford, blemished like us,
straddled a gravel
driveway
almost all the way
to the front porch at Ruby's

where a light
you could not help staring at
throbbed red as a cut
or lips
or July fruit. That light
was not yet a cliché.
It blushed
to lead us

where we would keep
watch for hours
inhaling the dark, swallowing
our voices
until everyone in the car
was silent as the dashboard clock,
too hot
to tell time.

Once we almost saw one

raise a window
which raised our hopes
and we swirled in powdered sheets,
tucked ourselves
like cash between rayon and flesh.
Mosquitoes whispered Bible verses.
Dime store perfume sprayed
sacred rituals
behind our ears,
Evening in Paris trickling
down our slim necks.

# TWO DREAMS DREAMED MORE THAN ONCE

So many times after Mother tucked me in,
my small body landscaping
the dark wool blanket, I'd dig again
rich soil behind our house.
Hands, deep in dirt, caught
coins loose as copper fish. Often
all I had to do was pick under shrubs
to scratch treasure. Nickels and pennies,
dimes luminescent as eyes,
I found beneath a forsythia
opening a million golden fingers
to shade me, keep me cool
under the hard spine of a morning sun.

My father's last summer
when Mother stared from her chair
like a winter flounder washed onto sand,
dreams reeked rusty water
rising, rising above my knees. I swam
sloping floors, felt the bite of a fish-
hook in the soft flesh inside my cheek.
And I sopped with a white dish towel
as if it were only cold milk spilled across a counter.

## IF ONLY SHE WILL PRACTICE

My father is teaching Mother
how to sign her name.
"Try, Peggy. You can do it.
It'll come back."
The sun has forgotten
to move across the window
and I can barely read the titles
of books in the shelves,
barely see my mother's pen
shuffle across the page
as if it were almost out of ink.
Her gray shoulders
lean into the table's curve.
If only she will practice long enough,
perhaps light will spring
through the window, dance around the room
like a child.

## MY MOTHER'S SHOES

Aunt Sarah never forgave her
for being Margaret.
Too many names
jammed Mother's dance cards,
hummed a tune
her sister could not
follow. The laugh, her eyes
the color of coffee
drew friends like a party.
My aunt tasted
Mother's beauty
from silver loving cups
lighting their dresser,
choking
as if a diamond ring
were caught in her throat.
Mother's romantic husband,
smocked children:
we even lived on Eden Terrace.
Today Aunt Sarah hauled off
all the shoes my mother left,
one size too small, determined
to wear them at last.

## MY FATHER'S HAT

A black and white
rough tweed
soft edges crushed
for comfort
squats on my bare closet shelf
like the hat that lay
on our choked brown yard
under a hard sun two days
after a snowfall
the icy body melted away
from under it.

## HUMORESQUE

Picture us dancing. Humoresque played
against stars set like rhinestones
in combs fastening my mother's cinnamon hair.
Brenda and I, sisters ruffled alike
in peach cotton, whirled as the moon
cracked into pieces and fell
over our shoulders like silver confetti.
Mother's white pumps followed my father's
turns around the Ocean Forest patio.
It was a summer the shape of gardenias.
The shape of a Wurlitzer jukebox.
Dancing Under the Stars, 1949.
Lips and fingernails were Revlon red,
organdy sundresses starched stiff
as company tablecloths. We were
ivory seashells arranging ourselves
on the sand, all the while
slipping closer and closer
to the heart of the sea.

# II. WILD BIRDS

# WHY I WANTED TO BE A FAMOUS DANCER

Understand I mean tap.
The dance of a stick
ticking off slats
in a picket fence.
The dance of a tongue
licking something cold
until it snaps.

You would watch me
enter the bloodlight
of the stage,
thousands of tiny sequins
all over me
raising the temperature
to smoke.
Not even you
could follow my feet
as they trip over
roots of music,
clapping like stars
in fiery circles
from one side of the stage
to the other.

And then
at exactly the right moment
I would stop,
the silence lifting everyone
from their seats,
making them laugh and cry
at the same time
and of course
as Kafka predicted,
the world would begin
to roll in ecstasy
at my feet.

## THE PASSIONATE SNAPSHOT
## OF MY FRIEND'S PARENTS

Lord, how they press into one another,
bodies joined like the lips of a slow smile.
Where his khaki ends, her printed cotton
begins. The embrace could break her back.

And they are not just kissing.
It's a war movie kiss. Like those I studied
from the Pix's velvet balcony, learned
by heart the way the woman tilted herself
up to the man, the way the man
took over. I breathe in

their biography, try to imagine
my own parents' faces on these young bodies,
let them shamelessly reach, enfold
and hold. The entire picture
delicious as an open mouth.

# AT A TABLE ACROSS FROM A CHILD

I carry a basket through the Casbah's
narrow streets, past the checkpoint
into the broad, leafy avenue.
I slip into a café packed with
breezy French colonels
and take a seat at a table
across from a small child
whose red sash has come undone.
She plays with her fork,
lays it down and presses her face
to her empty plate. Her mother reads.
I push my chair back to leave
and the child's fingers smooth the wrinkles
of her napkin. It could be the skin
of my cheek she is stroking. Or my arm
beneath the fabric of my sleeve.
Then slowly I rise, make my way
through the tables and chairs
of the crowded café, leaving
the basket behind. My footsteps
quicken to match my breath
and I am once again crossing the avenue,
its jewel-like colors rising
to meet me. Behind, the café
explodes like a single torch.
Objects. People. Pieces fan out,
then spin slowly through the air
like petals or stars
as if thousands of small worlds
were vanishing in one amazing cloud.
Red. Yellow. Purple. Orange.
It is every single color
a child could ever paint.

## PEOPLE WHOSE WIVES DIE

find someone else
before the silk of night
slips away, before the dirt settles
and sinks into the ground
around small flowers planted early.
They act as if they suddenly crossed over
from wind-cold shade straight to the sun.

Stay with me. It happens so fast
you cannot look away.

You'd think the sleet outside my window
was wedding rice, stones
from a bracelet. You'd think
the page these words run down was
pure linen or cotton to wrap across my eyes.

## MAYBE I WILL

lie beside you, trace the curve
of your fingernail
as if I were drawing
a picture or twisting lovely threads
or skimming the grooves of a record
we played last summer.

Maybe we will reason. Being more lawyer
than lover, we will weigh words
like fruit, unbutton our jackets of tweed
and lean back into logic.
A verdict will rise from our pipes
to circle our heads
and eventually fill the room.

Maybe I will scale you to the bone,
pick my teeth
with the fine splinters
of your spine. I will find
a wishbone in your elbow,
press my thumb and forefinger,
then pull, pull, pull
until I hear the beginnings
of rhythm.

## APOLOGY TO BOY CUTTING GRASS
## IN WEST TISBURY T-SHIRT

Most don't look like mine, I want to say
as you eyeball me through weathered

slats hiding me and my morning shower
from all of Martha's Vineyard. Some bellies

stay flat as the yards you work; thigh skin
stretches a tight fit. And some rumps

never slump nor fatten and flare
with expanding years. Your eyes

splash me cold as the spray I scrub under;
I picture all the younger bodies

you could be spying, should be eyeing
while your mower grinds that same strip

of lawn outside my shower back and forth,
back and forth, down to the dirt.

## ANOREXIC

Even your room is thin,
narrow bed
and fleshless chest
of drawers you open
with hands
so bony
each one claps.

I study your feet,
illumined x-rays.

Your dog
could bury you
in the yard,
saving sweet juice
for a dry afternoon.

Your ribs
make a perfect row,
teeth
in a plastic comb.
Your bones
a cage.

When nightshades
clothe your naked window
perhaps you pose
in a mirrored robe
of flesh
that minute to minute
swells
until you float
in the palm of your own hand
to a place
where clouds are scales
that weigh you in
at zero.

## RED SHOES

In my closet
they are planted
under the hems of my dresses
like poppies. When I wear them
I am someone else.
A nightclub comedian
sweating jokes, warming
the crowd for a star.

I am a child.
I skip cracks
as if they could open
like graves and suck me in
red shoes first.

I am third
from the left
in a line of dancers strutting
high-topped voices.
We kick our legs
like matches striking.
The stage catches fire
and a single color
sweeps across.

I fill an Amsterdam window
with cheap perfume,
raise higher
the dress
that matches my shoes.
My eyelashes are curled
tighter than the window-
shade. Later everything
slides down. The shade.
The sheets. And the dress.

# KEEPING THEIR SECRETS

She earned dimes at family reunions
rubbing an uncle's bald head.
His coins
tight as blisters
in her dark pocket.

How we all keep secrets
for uncles and others.

For the older brother who taught sister
a new game of poker
in mother's closet, the sleeves
of winter blouses teasing,
teasing. For the man next door

who showed books to neighborhood girls
behind the hedge. Leaves
from those books flying upward,
butterflies with badly-drawn wings
grazing the fence that separated
one yard from the other.

And fathers. The father
who eyed his daughter's frilled collar,
touching the lace
as if it were a leash,
as if it could simply melt
under the heat of his fingers
clear through to her throat.

We have practiced for years
how to keep their secrets,
how to keep from telling

until some night over a meal
one story, then another
will slip from our lips
like a name.

## MAD WOMAN

> I could chew up your entrails
> and dance on your bones.
> —what you said

How you would love to wrap my head
in muslin, circling me slowly
covering my eyes, my nose,
my mouth
until the whole world unravels
in a single gasp
and my last breath
is a snap of the fingers.
You dream of plunging my hand
into an urn of boiling liquid,
watching bubbles crawl between each finger,
lively ants learning the stubborn curves
of a skull. You would, of course,
pull my hand out in time
to smell parched flesh
as it begins to curl
in the coolness of the room.
You could stuff a cushion with hair
plucked from my head.
Sip my blood like tea.
Play my ribs, sing down the quiet center
of my spine.
Actually, anyone will do.
All that matters
is that you do to others
the kinds of things
your father did to you.

# LAYING ON OF HANDS

An evangelist is charged with
assaulting an ex-parishioner
by hitting him on the head
with a Bible.
— *The Charlotte Observer*

Let the word of God
penetrate your mind
take it into your heart
this kiss of peace
hallelujah
*blam*
I bring you
the treasury
of everlasting joy
the great world of light
sing praises
lift up your heart
your head if you can
*whack*
let the holy scriptures
show you the way
the good book
can lead you
in the paths
of righteousness
*splat*
take these glad tidings
I offer
this laying on of hands
my own revised version
of divine inspiration
and then
when I am through
try to stand up for Jesus.

## THIS MORNING'S CONVERSATION

Talking to you is the same
as stones falling on sand.
A bird's feather
licking the snow
in the sideyard. Car tires
spitting dried gravel
into dust, into pieces
of words I deliver
by the handful
to a vacant doorway
already filled
with last week's news.

# THE MOON HERSELF I COULD BE

I could be a moonflower
closing like window shutters
in merciless light. I would climb
porch posts, wrapping white
in ragged circles, until heart-leaves
shut out the lunchtime sun
and shadows double in heavy folds
like draperies. Every year the part of me
that springs from fertile soil
will die. Only my roots remain alive.

Or, I could be a moonstone
cut to celebrate June, permitting light
to elbow its way through,
almost as easily as glass.
All the while, I would reflect
the colors of blue to pearl
like a shawl slipping off someone's shoulders.

Or yes, the moon herself I could be,
pulling up the waters of earth
like a skirt I step into, yards of fabric
floating into my full-length mirror.
Water, rising and falling,
rising and falling, each time I choose
to turn my head upon the pillow
and face you.

## WILD BIRDS

I like to think that anything
is possible. Look at me,
a breath holder,
a person well-armored in forms
and channels, caught in the short orbit
of an orderly world. Surely
I can escape

with serious practice, of course,

to a time when I will begin to sing
an accidental song,
peel a tangerine
the color of my hair,
take scissors to the straps
of the sweet-smelling gown I wear,

open my door suddenly to wild birds.

# III. HOLDING BACK WINTER

## SUICIDE

The newspaper lied.
They did not find you
on the floor. Instead
you spent the afternoon
pitching with your son,
your face catching the silence
of the yard
like a soft leather glove
lovingly broken in.
And the light, the remarkable light,
ran over you so carelessly
it looked like silver numbers on your shirt.
You threw the ball for hours
as if there were no chance
night would ever search the corners
like the crowd
finding places in the stands,
their eyes marking the hard mound of dirt
below. For hours.
As if there were nothing at all
left to explain.

## HANDLING THE SERPENTS

> They will pick up serpents
> and . . . it will not hurt them;
> they will lay their hands on the sick
> and they will recover.
>                 —Mark 16: 17-18

And now we come to bury
Brother Charles
who pulled snakes
from his pulpit
as if it were a holy
hat, as if those serpents
had long white ears
instead of fangs
to hear the prayers
spoken in tongues,
thin, flicking tongues
so forked
they rattled
the Apostolic Church of God
six miles
from the slag heaps
of the old Isabella
Copper Mine.
Copperheads slid up
his wrist,
coiled his arm,
his neck and cheek
one too many times.
Brother Charles' blood
cooled
at a church member's home
till it was time
for him to pass
the winter
deep in the earth

beneath blue
and orange carnations
banding his casket
in slender ribbons.
The accordian player
squeezes out
Amazing Grace,
seems he's wheezing
one last breath.
Chords
hang
in the tin roof heat
like tubes of skin
slipped off.
And we recall
Brother Charles
who wanted to go
when the Lord
got through with him
and the Lord
got through with him
just after
we fixed our eyes
on the billed cap
he always wore
and the
Canebrake rattlesnake
starting to circle
four words
printed across
the crown:
In God We Trust.

## READING AT BEDTIME

> Then a tremendous flash of light
> cut across the sky.
> 
> —*Hiroshima*
>   by John Hersey

On the cover, clouds stack
like a soft sandcastle
dripping, reaching higher and higher
as if it were building
a monument to itself.

First chapter. "A Noiseless Flash."
I suck in my lips,
read, put down the book, read,
turn myself to face the light,
then pull my covers up around me
like skin I can count on.

There is no relief between the words,
only the sound of pages turning.
I reach toward the lamp
and my room seems suddenly far away
in the darkness.

Now I am dreaming and there is water.
My son, younger even than he is today,
swims toward a shore
he can never reach
and of course, the enemy.
They surround him,
sending their flashes to skip the water
like small rocks my son and I hurled
across the lake last December.
The enemy is laughing
and I remember how we laughed
at the rocks I'd skipped
which never traveled far enough
no matter how I tried.

I am screaming to my son
to remain underwater, to dip
into air as little as possible
when suddenly I am the one in water
whose outspread arms will not move me along.
I have traveled so far
my breaths come like waves
and still I swim into my son
who swims into my body which rolls over
in the glow of early morning light
flashing silently
through my bedroom window.

## MEDICINE WOMEN
## DOING WHAT WE HAVE TO DO

I whip the thermometer against fevered
air in my daughter's room, carve a sliver
of cool with that whit whit whit
as mercury runs down the slender tube,
streaking lightless corners.
Buried deep in scarlet wool, she stares

at my arm, as I remember fixing
parched eyes on my mother's arm
shaking in time to the same ritual.
I have read that mothers,
their ancient stone tools colder
than my glass wand, once carved
holes in the skull to release

spirits. Some mothers, their skin
dark as bad news, waited out a fever
plunging deep beneath the mattress,
tucking in a knife to cut the pain.
Indian mothers painted sun gods
as if burning sand were a suitable canvas

to stretch healing across the grains.
Poultice strong enough to stop
the breath still buries
children's chests like water
chilled to the touch, like the palm
of a wind-cold hand
or a mother's face.

## SUCKED INTO THE TUNNEL
## MY DAUGHTER TRAVELS

I ride her roller coaster
and scream her screams.

We finger the neon afternoon
while our arms wave back fear.
The trick is to keep hands high
as if we get more credit

when we don't hold on.

The box we share
drops faster than we
can breathe. Then slowly, slowly

it pulls us up the next
perfect hill and we open our faces
to whatever comes next.
Are we having fun? Are we laughing?
Maybe snapshots will tell

long after the traces of our bond
give in to gravity.

## ADOLESCENCE

When the words have all been eaten
and the mouths of little babies open
and open like ladies singing opera or fish
flapping their fins just under a Saran surface
singing who got my food
and even when something is said
sentences end before the period
as if some stop sign shot up
and all that's left are burning puddles
of things implied,
she sucks in her breath
with dark sounds. I think they are cries.

## ACTUALLY SHE DID NOT ANSWER

Said she'd only heard me
from a corner of her mind.

I know that place.
An empty sleeve, a slice
of plastic for a billfold
face. That space

narrow as the pocket
my hands would form in prayer
if I prayed that way.
Scattered in the room
of my daughter's mind

are weeks of secrets.
They collect like laundry,
still smell like
skin. If I could

climb in there
I'd be busy
sewing buttons tighter,
matching sock
to sock, finding

lost dimes and smoothing
down the wrinkles.

# FOLLOWING MY DAUGHTER

Here we are in separate cars

staying as tight together
as album pages closed. You know the way

and I follow, through uneven light
that turns the trees
and houses beside the road
pale and wavy, distant as a snapshot.

I love how you now lead,
your ability to make your way
with the only companion you need:
the breathless music you make.

I take the turns you take

remembering another time I followed
but actually ran beside you

my hand holding the seat
of your two-wheel bike
until it was suddenly free
and I could no longer run fast enough

and there you were
riding wild without me
the front wheel dipping left
then right and you
laughing yourself straight and steady
down the street as far as I could see.

# EVEN WHEN WE ARE TOGETHER

I have tried to write you
into the lines of my poems
but when I visit childhood
you are not there.
My brother, eight years older
and more years than that removed,
you were the one
who did not look like either parent,
as if you emerged from the woods next door.

How can I tell you about distance?
We talk on the phone
and I laugh when I ask
if you are reading
while we speak.
Even when we are together,
you disappear into your jokes
and all that's left is a punch line.

I keep looking in your face,
try to stare down the aloneness
but you are still the oldest
so I let you have your way.

Each time, I am sure it will be different.
I wave my hands like an evangelist,
shaking out words
that eventually settle and ice over
and soon we are both protected
by a glaze, transparent as ever,
and we sit beside each other,
smiling and mute.

## THE CONTEST

We are sisters playing Scrabble,
clicking our tiles
like tongues. Something in the way
we play our hands says "what if I lose?
what if I don't?" We reach

across the board signing our story
as if we cannot hear, place words
precisely so each letter
fills one space. Make sure
they never brush or bump each other.

See how our words
lock patterns, shaping right angles
so straight they will not give.
Behind walls of wood we shift
vowels and consonants
until time runs out, until they spell

exactly what we want.
What we need to say takes more
than seven letters, more
than either of us has drawn.
I take a turn. You take
a turn. And as long as the game goes on,
careful as accountants, we keep score.

# ANSWERS I KNOW CAN NEVER BE RIGHT

> People have the examination dream
> when they face some significant
> life stress. It is actually an
> attempt to reassure oneself.
>
>      — Andrew Pickens, psychiatrist

I listen for the clock to clear its throat
and dread the teacher's stockinged legs
beside my desk, imagine her
plucking the pages from my hands
as if she were collecting quarters.
The questions change.
They dance over my paper like a child
whose face appears in unlikely places.
I chew the tip of my pencil,
erase the answers I know can never be right
and brush away eraser dust
that spots my paper like confusion.
The others have all gone home.
I sign my name above the date and know
I've stayed too long. Even the bells
hold their breath. Men in dark overalls
are sponging down the blackboards,
mopping the floors until they are so slick
a person can barely keep balance.

## A MOTHER, RAGING

This is a henhouse

and I am the farmer
whose heavy boots
splinter the floorboards.
Watch me enter, waving

my butcherknife,
a silver flag with an edge

sharper than cracked shells.
I am pleased to see such slim necks
and of course, eggs

too fresh not to eat.

Now the chickens
are screaming
and fussing their feathers
until the whole place shakes

and delicate pieces of white
ruffle the room, disturb
the early morning

like naked bulbs
switched on and left swinging.

## INSULT FROM A GYNECOLOGIST

Legs pulled, split into a Sunday wishbone,
I slide forward at the nurse's request
closer to the end, wondering
if anyone ever slipped
too far, over the edge
in the spirit of cooperation.
Trained in origami
or Maypole, she weaves a sheet
in and out my curves and corners
until I am a table draped in white damask
ready to receive guests. Here
there are no candles. A penlight
will do. Long-awaited visitor

enters the room, his hands washed clean
as silverware and other narrow instruments.
He lowers himself to a chrome stool.
Like a union man bellying up to the bar,
he wheels in closer, finally arrives
at the banquet. I peek through
the open triangle my legs form
to catch him in the act of yawning.

# HOLDING BACK WINTER

Blame it on the ginkgo leaves,
those October coins
tossed like rings or kisses
all around us.
We did not need the sun.
My face bright, a morning wish,
as I posed for your picture,
my hair browner than the bark
you caught behind me.

This very minute
I would press myself flat,
pull us both
into the snapshot
like film run backwards
drawing people back
where they once were.

There. Now we both
lean against the fence,
lean into the camera,
our eyes wide
as small suns.

How the yellow light
holds back winter,
freezes autumn
as if it were a young couple
just starting out,
before they can learn
the crusted winds
that sweep one life into the next.
That young married couple
smiling their hearts out
for a souvenir.

Judy Goldman grew up in Rock Hill, South Carolina, and now writes and teaches poetry in Charlotte, North Carolina. Her poems have appeared in numerous periodicals and have won many prizes and awards.